NICKELODEON

SpongeBob SquarePants

TRIVIA
BOOK

*Stephen Hillenburg*

Based on the TV series *SpongeBob SquarePants* ® created by Stephen Hillenburg
as seen on Nickelodeon ®

SIMON SPOTLIGHT
An imprint of Simon & Schuster Children's Publishing Division
1230 Avenue of the Americas, New York, New York 10020

Manufactured in the United States of America

First Edition
8 10 9 7

ISBN 0-689-84018-7

NICKELODEON

SpongeBob™ squarepants

TRIVIA BOOK

BY
DAVID FAIN

Simon Spotlight/Nickelodeon

New York      London      Toronto      Sydney      Singapore

# TABLE of CONTENTS

Avast there, mateys! Here's the rarest sea creature of them all—SpongeBob SquarePants! He may look like an ordinary sponge to you landlubbers, but take my word for it, he's the most unique talking yellow cube filled with holes you'll ever find on the ocean floor— or any floor for that matter.

# I'm READy

Hi! I'm SpongeBob SquarePants! And I'm ready to start another wonderful day here in Bikini Bottom. I'm ready, I'm ready, I'm ready! Whoops! Look at the time! I still have to do my morning workout, eat a healthy breakfast of Kelpo, and feed my pet snail, Gary, before I go to work.

# ·RIENDS and NEIGHBORS

I've got lots of neat friends. Let me introduce you to some of them.

Patrick is my best friend. We do everything together: jellyfishing, blowing bubbles, playing superheroes, hunting ·· pirate treasure, you name it. He also likes sleeping, drooling, and lying dormant under his rock.

Sandy is a land squirrel, which means she has to wear a hat full of air and a pressure suit to live underwater. She's a great surfer and an excellent karate expert, just like me! She's from this faraway place called Texas. That's why she talks the way she does. Don't worry, you get used to it after a while.

That's my next door neighbor, Squidward Tentacles. Even though we work all day together at the Krusty Krab, I never get tired of spending time with him. He practices his clarinet a lot, although he never seems to get any better. He doesn't have time to play with Patrick and me. We practically have to drag him out of his house kicking and screaming just to get him to have some fun.

Mr. Krabs is my boss, and the owner of the Krusty Krab restaurant where Squidward and I work. People say he's cheap, but I consider it an honor to work for the creator of the Krabby Patty! Sometimes I think that maybe I should be paying him!

# AROUND BIKINI BOTTOM

Patrick's rock

two-story pineapple

Easter Island head

Here's where we live. The two-story pineapple is mine. It's fully equipped with a shellphone, state of the art stuffed animal barbells, and a foghorn alarm clock. Next door is my pal Squidward's Easter Island head, and next to that is my friend Patrick's rock. Every weekend I use my reef blower to keep my yard seashell free and sparkling.

Howdy, y'all! This is my house, the treedome! It's full of the driest, purest, airyest air in the whole sea! I have all the comforts of home: an exercise wheel, a picnic table, an oak tree, and a trampoline. The treedome is made of polyurethane (that's a fancy name for plastic).

# BORN to COOK

Here it is, my work place, the finest eating establishment ever established for eating—the Krusty Krab! Home of that tasty, juicy, scrumptious, warm mouthful of steamy goodness called the Krabby Patty! Would you like fries with that?

Across the street is the Chum Bucket, owned by Mr. Krabs's archrival, Plankton! With the help of his computer, Karen, Plankton's always trying to steal the Krabby Patty recipe. People say he's evil, but I think he just needs a friend.

It's not that easy to become a member of the Krusty
crew. You really need the expertise to properly
prepare the perfect Krabby Patty.

First comes the bun, then the patty,
followed by ketchup, mustard, pickles, onions,
lettuce, cheese, tomatoes and bun—
in that order.

# THE RENAISSANCE CEPHALOPOD

Hello, friends, and welcome to my private art gallery. I have conquered all artistic mediums in my pursuit of the perfect self-portrait. Being the only squid of culture in this backward community is a heavy burden, but one I could gladly bear if it weren't for the constant pestering of . . . SPONGEBOB SQUAREPANTS! I can't get a moment's peace from that nuisance and his equally annoying friend Patrick!

Do you know they come over every day (and twice on Sundays) to ask me if I want to go jellyfishing? Jellyfishing? Me? Have you ever heard of anything so ridiculous?!

And that's just the beginning! SpongeBob throws me birthday parties when it's not my birthday,

he's always making a racket,

and as if that isn't bad enough, he keeps leaving his undergarments on my front lawn!

# BUBBLE-BLOWING TECHNIQUE

Wanna blow some bubbles? It only costs twenty-five cents. Here's your bubble wand, dipped and ready to go. Remember, it's all in the technique!

* First, go like this.
* Spin around—stop!
* Double-take three times . . . one, two, and three.
* Pelvic Thrust—Woo Hoo!
* Stomp on your right foot. (Don't forget it!)
* Now it's time to bring it around town. Bring it around town!
* Then you do this, then this, and this and that and thisandthatandthisandthat!

You can blow bubbles in all sorts of interesting shapes.
Try some of these:

A CUBE
DUCKS          A DANCE PARTNER
A CENTIPEDE        A TUGBOAT
A BUTTERFLY        AN ELEPHANT

You can also whisper messages inside the bubbles to send to your friends. Just be sure the right person gets the right message. Or that the message is from the right person. Or that the message goes to the person on your right. Or that you don't forget . . . oh, tartar sauce! I forgot who I was sending this message to!

# CHAMPIONS
## of the DEEP

You're just in time for my favorite television show: *The Adventures of MermaidMan!* I've got a genuine imitation copy of his uniform. Patrick says his young ward, Barnacle Boy, is better, but that's just because that's who he is when we play superheroes.

They are so cool!
Patrick and I found
out that MermaidMan and
Barnacle Boy live over at the
Shady Shoals older citizens' home.
We think they're working undercover!

Recently roused from retirement, the aquatic avengers have launched a new series of adventures, though now much older (and considerably less wiser). Watch in awe as they:

CHANGE A LIGHTBULB!

WAIT FOR THE
AQUAPHONE REPAIRMAN!

EAT THEIR MEATLOAF!

ADJUST THEIR
HEARING AIDS!

PLAY CHECKERS!

TRY TO REMEMBER
WHERE THEY PARKED THE
INVISIBLE BOATMOBILE!

# BOATING SCHOOL QUIZ

When I'm not working, I go to Mrs. Puff's Boating School. I can hardly wait until I get my license. If only I didn't always get so nervous during the driving exam. Oh well, you know what they say—thirty-eighth time's the charm! (Okay, thirty-ninth!)

Mrs. Puff is the best boating teacher I've ever had. Well, actually she's the only boating teacher I've ever had. She's a puffer fish (which means she has her own built in airbag, which comes in very handy during those driving tests). Let's see how much you know about boating:

**1** The front of the boat is called the
a) bow.
b) porthole.
c) stern.

**2** The first thing you do when you're about to start the driving test is
a) floor it!
b) put it in drive.
c) start the boat.

**3** Red means
a) floor it!
b) stop.
c) make a right turn.

**4** If you see a big anchor in the middle of the road, you should
a) floor it!
b) crash into it.
c) jump over it.

**5** The second thing you do when you're taking the driving test is
a) pop a wheelie.
b) put it in drive.
c) cross the finish line.

**6** If you see someone in the crosswalk while you're driving, you should
a) get out and help him or her cross the street.
b) turn around and go the other way.
c) go upside down.

**7** In boating terms, right is
a) starboard.
b) port.
c) wrong.

**8** If your boat has a kitchen onboard it's called
a) the keel.
b) the hall monitor.
c) the galley.

**9** If you have a walkie-talkie inside your head and someone else is telling you what to do during the driving test, you are
a) lucky.
b) dreaming.
c) cheating.

**10** The last thing you should do when you're taking the driving test is
a) watch Mrs. Puff being taken away in an ambulance.
b) cross the finish line.
c) floor it!

ANSWERS:
1A, 2C, 3B, 4C, 5B, 6A, 7A, 8C, 9C, 10B

# SQUIDWARD SEZ

Our pal Squidward is always claiming that he doesn't want to play with SpongeBob and me. We know he's just playing a game where he says the opposite of what he really means (just like on Opposite Day). Let me show you. First he'll talk, and then I'll translate.

## WHEN SQUIDWARD SAYS:

"How did I ever get surrounded by such loser neighbors?"

## HE REALLY MEANS:

"I have the best neighbors in the world!"

## WHEN SQUIDWARD SAYS:

"You're killing me, SpongeBob . . . you really are!"

## HE REALLY MEANS:

"Do it again!"

## WHEN SQUIDWARD SAYS:

"Can we lower the volume, please?"

## HE REALLY MEANS:

"Do it again . . . louder!"

## WHEN SQUIDWARD SAYS:

"Oh, puh-leez!"

## HE REALLY MEANS:

"You're welcome."

# WHO SAID IT?

Hear me, surface dwellers! That simpleton starfish isn't the only one around here who knows something about language! I have created a foolproof device that allows me to perfectly imitate the voice of any resident of Bikini Bottom I choose! Don't ask how this will help me to obtain a Krabby Patty—it's far too complicated to explain to your miniscule mentalities. What I need from you is help in sorting out who says what! Match each sentence to the person most likely to have said it, and I may spare you when I destroy this miserable town!

1 "Mother O' Pearl!"

2 "Sea creatures assemble!"

3 "Is it already time to ruin Squid's day?"

4 "Meow."

5 "Ain't that just the bee's knees?"

6 "You guys want to lift some weights?"

7 "I'm ready!"

8 "Oh, my aching tentacles!"

9 "Daddy, you're embarrassing me!"

10 "Whose turn is it to be hall monitor?"

A SpongeBob

B Patrick

C Sandy

D Squidward

E Mr. Krabs

F MermaidMan

G Gary

H Larry the Lobster

I Mrs. Puff

J Pearl

25

# MUSSEL BEACH PARTY

This is Mussel Beach, where my friends and I sometimes go to have fun. Everyone has their own favorite things to do here, and at the nearby, wonderful, stinky mud puddle we call Goo Lagoon. I'll let them tell you themselves!

Well, I get really stoked from catching a wave! That's surfing, for all you nonaquatic wannabes. My favorite move is to do a handstand while shooting the tube. That way I can hang ten ... fingers that is! I also enjoy playing Frisbee with my friends, although SpongeBob tends to try catching it with his face!

What I like doing at Goo Lagoon is lying on the sand and sleeping. Actually I like lying on the sand and sleeping anywhere. I don't even have to be on sand ... or even lying down. I just ... like ... zzz zzz zzz.

Well, if I wasn't always being bothered by certain very annoying people, I would luxuriate in working on my tan at Mussel Beach.

As for me, I like hanging out in the juice bar, singing beach music, and playing in the sand. But here are a few activities you want to avoid if you don't want to end up the biggest loser on the beach:

- ⊘ Getting sand in your buns
- ⊘ Forgetting your sunscreen (and getting sunburned)
- ⊘ Being buried in the sand and getting left behind
- ⊘ Ripping your pants (repeatedly)
- ⊘ Pretending to drown

# MAY I TAKE YOUR ORDER

THE KRUSTY KRAB, HOME OF THE ONE AND ONLY KRABBY PATTY!

Remember, at the Krusty Krab,

YOU ARE THE CAPTAIN!

## SANDWICHES

$2.00

KRABBY PATTY

$2.50

DOUBLE KRABBY PATTY
WITH THE WORKS

KRUSTY COMBO KRABBY PATTY, FRIES, AND MEDIUM DRINK

$3.99

$3.00

KRUSTY DELUXE
DOUBLE KRABBY PATTY
WITH THE WORKS AND OYSTER SKINS

**CRYING JOHNNIE** **$2.25**
KRABBY PATTY
WITH EXTRA ONIONS

**$1.99**

**BUBBLE BASS SPECIAL**
KRABBY PATTY HOLD THE PICKLES
(UNDER YOUR TONGUE)

**$1.75**

**MINNOW MEAL**
SEANUT BUTTER AND JELLYFISH JELLY
SANDWICH, FRIES, AND SMALL DRINK

## SIDES

OYSTER SKINS . . . . . . . . . . . . . . . . . . . . . . . . . . . $.50
FRIES . . . . . . . . . . . . . . . . . . . . . . . . . . . . . . . $1.25
SEAWEED SALAD . . . . . . . . . . . . . . . . . . . . . . . . $1.50
CORAL BITS . . . . . . . . . . . . . . . . . . . . . . . . . . . $1.95

## DRINKS

**SALTY SHAKES** **$.99**     **DR. KELP OR DIET DR. KELP** **$.89**

And don't forget, every Tuesday is Mouthful of Clams Day! Everyone who shows up with a mouthful of clams gets a free drink!

## MONEY BACK GUARANTEE

# THE SECRETS to SUCCESSFUL JELLYFISHING

Welcome to Jellyfish Fields, where wild jellyfish roam, just waiting to be captured. This is the best place in Bikini Bottom to go jellyfishing. Here are a few pointers for you beginners:

☺ Bring a good solid net. Be sure to name it. Mine's called "Ol' Reliable."

☺ Remember, SAFETY FIRST! Always wear your safety glasses.

☺ Firmly grasp the net.

☺ Always set the jellyfish free after you've caught it (you wouldn't like being kept in a jar either).

☺ It helps if you sing "La, la, la" or "Da, da, da, da dum" while you jellyfish.

☺ Disguise yourself as a piece of coral in order to get close to your prey.

☺ Watch out for those stingers!

The jellyfish who live in Bikini Bottom are completely different from all other jellyfish in the sea. For example, they make a loud buzzing sound when they swim, they live in hives, and produce a delicious strawberry-flavored jelly. There's nothing like the taste of natural jelly from a jellyfish.

Remember: these jellyfish aren't pets, they're wild animals. They have powerful electrical stingers and use them when angry. They love to dance, and can't resist a good solid beat. But be warned: they don't like clarinet music (at least they don't like the way Squidward plays clarinet music)!

33

# SPONGEBOB'S BUSY SCHEDULE

Sometimes I have so much to do it's hard to keep it straight. I'm glad I've got someplace to write it all down!

## Sunday 10

Opposite Day. Be sure to act like Squidward.

## Monday 11

Boating Exam today— don't forget to bring apple for Mrs. Puff. (Some band-ages might not be a bad idea either.)

## Friday 15

15th of the month . . . Annoy Squidward Day! Call Patrick.

## Saturday 16

Squidward's Birthday!

## Sunday 17

Annual Jellyfish Convention in Ukulele Bottom. Find snail-sitter for Gary.

## Tuesday 19

Have Squidward cover as fry cook. Make sure Krusty Krab is well-stocked with antacid tablets before leaving. Buy Mr. Krabs a gift to make up for loss in profits.

## Wednesday 20

Squidward's Birthday!

## Thursday 21

Glove World Grand Opening! Remind Patrick we need to stand in line all weekend to be sure we are the very first ones inside, just like last year.

## Saturday 23

Sign Up Deadline for Mussel Beach Anchor Throw. Make sure to keep Sandy occupied and far away from Goo Lagoon. Prepare karate ambush?

## Sunday 24

Squidward's Birthday!

## Tuesday 26

Employee of the Month Judging Begins. Break Squidward's alarm clock.

## Wednesday 27

Anniversary of first Day met Sandy. Definitely prepare karate ambush! Pay day. Buy Mr. Krabs a sympathy card.

## Friday 29

Squidward's Birthday!

# SNAIL CARE

Meow!

Okay, I'll tell them, G
Gary wants me to let
know the most impor
information in the care
feeding of pet snails:

**1.** Snails need lots of food. They get one can of snail food in the morning and one can at night.

**2.** Don't let them get salty. Make sure they have plenty of water.

**3.** They need to be walked twice a day.

**4.** Snails love to play "fetch." Bring something to read, this can take awhile.

**5.** Your pet snail's "meowing" at the moon can annoy the neighbors. Try to keep it to a minimum.

**6.** Snails are natural-born poets. Encourage their artistic expression.

**7.** VERY, VERY IMPORTANT: Whatever you do, don't let yourself get accidentally injected with snail plasma.

# DANGERS of the DEPTHS

Howdy, y'all. As Bikini Bottom's resident science expert, I'm here to tell y'all about a few sea critters you should give a wide berth to should they ever cross yer path:

Giant Clam. I tussled with one of these rascals myself the first time SpongeBob and I met. They're just big bullies. A few well-placed karate chops will more'n likely send them on their way with their tails betwixt their legs (if'n they had any legs, that is).

Nematodes (or undersea worms). These hungry little dudes don't look like much, but put a passel of them together and they can gnaw a coral reef down to a stub in ten seconds flat.

**The Mother of All Jellyfish.** This is the large economy-sized version of those cute little fellers who float out in Jellyfish Fields. But this mamma packs quite a wallop when it comes to stingers. Just ask Squidward.

**Anchovies.** Just like nematodes these little dudes ain't anything to be afraid of in small numbers, but fill a few tour buses with schools of these hungry fish, and they're as likely to stampede as look at ya! And to top it off, they're smellier than all get out.

**Poison Sea Urchins.** They're tiny and spiny and make you itch all over.

**The Flying Dutchman.** Although technically not a critter, he's more of a bogeyman ghost-type varmint. Anyhoo, he's as ornery as Mr. Krabs on payday and twice as ugly, so keep yer distance or he'll steal yer soul!

# DID YOU KNOW?

Did you know that in Bikini Bottom—

⊙ Moss always points to civilization.

❀ Through the misuse of time travel, Squidward invented the art of jellyfishi

⊙ The specialty of the house at Plankton's restaurant, The Chum Bucket, is Chumbalaya. (No wonder he doesn't have any customers!)

❀ SpongeBob has won the employee of the month award twenty-six months in a row.

⊙ The Flying Dutchman haunts the Seven Seas because he was never put to rest (people used his body for a window display after he died).

✳ In the future, everything will be chrome and there will be 486 letters in the alphabet (one for each SpongeTron clone produced).

☺ Patrick knows a lot about head injuries.

✳ Mr. Krabs has an acute sense of smell.

☺ SpongeBob has had the following items inside his head:

-A towel

-Plankton

-A walkie-talkie

-A lightbulb
(He makes a pretty good disco ball.)

✳ Squidward has a lifetime subscription to *Frown Digest Magazine*.

☺ Souls look like pickles.

✳ SpongeBob also plays a mean conch.

Did y'all know that up in the surface world . . .

✳ SpongeBob SquarePants series creator Stephen Hillenburg has a degree in marine biology as well as experimental animation.

☺ SpongeBob was originally named SpongeBoy, but someone was already using that name, so the "y" became a "b."

✻ Ernest Borgnine and Tim Conway provide the voices for MermaidMan and Barnacle Boy. This is the first time the two have worked together since *McHale's Navy*.

☺ Staff writer Mr. Lawrence contributes spoken as well as written words for the series. He performs the voice of Mr. Krabs's archrival Plankton, the announcer at sporting events in Goo Lagoon, and several others. (He's also the voice of Philbert the turtle on *Rocko's Modern Life*).

✻ Painty the Pirate (seen at the beginning of each SpongeBob SquarePants episode singing the theme song) has the live-action lips of series creator Stephen Hillenburg.

# SING ALONG with PAINTY

Ahoy there, Kids! Ready to sing the SpongeBob SquarePants theme song?

I can't hear you!

OOOOOOOOOOOOOOOOOH, Who lives in a pineapple under the sea?
SpongeBob SquarePants!
Absorbent and yellow and porous is he.
SpongeBob SquarePants!
If nautical nonsense be something you wish,
SpongeBob SquarePants!
Then drop on the deck and flop like a fish!
SpongeBob SquarePants!
SpongeBob SquarePants!
SpongeBob SquarePants!
SpongeBob SquarePants!
Sponge–   Bob, Square–  Pants!
Ah ha ha ha  ah har har har

## 1 GRAND PRIZE:
A 3-day/2-night trip for four to Nickelodeon Studios in Orlando, Florida

## 3 FIRST PRIZES:
A Sony Playstation® system and a *Rugrats™ in Paris* Playstation game from THQ®

## 25 SECOND PRIZES:
A *The Wild Thornberrys* CD-ROM from Mattel Interactive

## 100 THIRD PRIZES:
A set of four books from Simon & Schuster Children's Publishing, including a *The Wild Thornberrys* title, a *Rugrats* title, a *SpongeBob SquarePants* title, and a *Hey Arnold!* title

Complete entry form and send to:
Simon & Schuster Children's Publishing Division
Marketing Department/ "Nickelodeon Studios Florida Sweepstakes"
1230 Avenue of the Americas, 4th Floor, NY, NY 10020

Name_____ Birthdate___/___/_____

Address_____

City_____ State_____ Zip_____

Phone ( ____ ) _____

Parent/Guardian Signature _____

See back for official rules.

Simon Spotlight Books

NICKELODEON

NICKELODEON STUDIOS

THQ

MATTEL INTERACTIVE

# Simon & Schuster Children's Publishing Division/ "Nickelodeon Studios Florida Sweepstakes" Sponsor's Official Rules:

NO PURCHASE NECESSARY.

Enter by mailing this completed Official Entry Form (no copies allowed) or by mailing a 3 1/2" x 5" card with your complete name and address, parent and/or legal guardian's name, daytime telephone number, and birthdate to the Simon & Schuster Children's Publishing Division/ "Nickelodeon Studios Florida Sweepstakes," 1230 Avenue of the Americas, 4th Floor, NY, NY 10020. Entry forms are available in the back of *The Rugrats Files #3: The Quest for the Holey Pail* (12/2000), *Rugrats Chapter Book #10: Dil in a Pickle* (11/2000), *The Wild Thornberrys Chapter Book #2: Two Promises Too Many!* (9/2000), *The Wild Thornberrys Chapter Book #3: A Time to Share* (9/2000), *SpongeBob SquarePants Trivia Book* (9/2000), *SpongeBob SquarePants Joke Book* (9/2000), *Hey Arnold! Chapter Book #1: Arnold for President* (9/2000), and *Hey Arnold! Chapter Book #2: Return of the Sewer King* (9/2000), and on the web site SimonSaysKids.com. Sweepstakes begins 8/1/2000 and ends 2/28/2001. Entries must be postmarked by 2/28/01 and received by 3/15/01. Not responsible for lost, late, damaged, postage-due, stolen, illegible, mutilated, incomplete, or misdirected or not delivered entries or mail, or for typographical errors in the entry form or rules. Entries are void if they are in whole or in part illegible, incomplete, or damaged. Enter as often as you wish, but each entry must be mailed separately. Entries will not be returned. Winners will be selected at random from all eligible entries received in a drawing to be held on or about 3/30/01. Grand prize winner must be available to travel during the months of June and July 2001. If Grand Prize winner is unable to travel on the specified dates, prize will be forfeited and awarded to an alternate. Winners will be notified by mail within 30 days of selection. The grand prize winner will be notified by phone as well. Odds of winning depend on the number of eligible entries received.

Prizes: One Grand Prize: A 3-day/2-night trip for four to Nickelodeon Studios in Orlando, FL, including a VIP tour, admission for four to Universal Studios Florida, round-trip coach airfare from a major U.S. airport nearest the winner's residence, and standard hotel accommodations (2 rooms, double occupancy) of sponsor's choice. (Total approx. retail value: $2,700.00). Winner must be accompanied by a parent or legal guardian. Prize does not include transfers, gratuities, or any other expenses not specified or listed herein. 3 First Prizes: A Sony Playstation system and a *Rugrats* Playstation game from THQ. (Total approx. retail value: $150.00 each). 25 Second Prizes: A *The Wild Thornberrys* CD-ROM from Mattel Interactive. (Approx. retail value: $29.99 each). 100 Third Prizes: A set of four books from Simon & Schuster Children's Publishing, including a *The Wild Thornberrys* title, a *Rugrats* title, a *SpongeBob SquarePants* title, and a *Hey Arnold!* title. (Total approx. retail value: $12.00 per set).

The sweepstakes is open to legal residents of the continental U.S. (excluding Puerto Rico) and Canada (excluding Quebec) ages 5-13 as of 2/28/01. Proof of age is required to claim prize. Prizes will be awarded to winner's parent or legal guardian. Void wherever prohibited or restricted by law. All provincial, federal, state, and local laws apply. Simon & Schuster Inc. and MTV Networks and their respective officers, directors, shareholders, employees, suppliers, parent companies, subsidiaries, affiliates, agencies, sponsors, participating retailers, and persons connected with the use, marketing, or conducting of this sweepstakes are not eligible. Family members living in the same household as any of the individuals referred to in the preceding sentence are not eligible.

One prize per person or household. Prizes are not transferable, have no cash equivalent, and may not be substituted except by sponsors, in the event of prize unavailability, in which case a prize of equal or greater value will be awarded. All prizes will be awarded.

If a winner is a Canadian resident, then he/she must correctly answer a skill-based question administered by mail.

All expenses on receipt and use of prize including provincial, federal, state, and local taxes are the sole responsibility of the winner's parent or legal guardian. Winners' parents or legal guardians may be required to execute and return an Affidavit of Eligibility and Publicity Release and all other legal documents which the sweepstakes sponsors may require (including a W-9 tax form) within 15 days of attempted notification or an alternate winner will be selected. The grand prize winner, parent or legal guardian, and travel companions will be required to execute a liability release form prior to ticketing.

Winners' parents or legal guardians on behalf of the winners agree to allow use of winners' names, photographs, likenesses, and entries for any advertising, promotion, and publicity purposes without further compensation to or permission from the entrants, except where prohibited by law.

Winners and winners' parents or legal guardians agree that Simon & Schuster, Inc., Nickelodeon Studios, THQ, and MTV Networks and their respective officers, directors, shareholders, employees, suppliers, parent companies, subsidiaries, affiliates, agencies, sponsors, participating retailers, and persons connected with the use, marketing, or conducting of this sweepstakes shall have no responsibility or liability for injuries, losses, or damages of any kind in connection with the collection, acceptance, or use of the prizes awarded herein, or from participation in this promotion.

By participating in this sweepstakes, entrants agree to be bound by these rules and the decisions of the judges and sweepstakes sponsors, which are final in all matters relating to the sweepstakes. Failure to comply with the Official Rules may result in a disqualification of your entry and prohibition of any further participation in this sweepstakes.

The first names of the winners will be posted at SimonSaysKids.com or the first names of the winners may be obtained by sending a stamped, self-addressed envelope after 3/30/01 to Prize Winners, Simon & Schuster Children's Publishing Division "Nickelodeon Studios Sweepstakes," 1230 Avenue of the Americas, 4th Floor, NY, NY 10020.

Sponsor of sweepstakes is Simon & Schuster Inc.